i Hate Reading*

* How to get through 20 minutes of reading a day
without really reading.

By Arthur and Henry Bacon

Illustrated by Johanna Hantel

Fort Atkinson, Wisconsin
www.upstartbooks.com

Scene 1

OK. You have to read for
20 minutes. But you don't
want to. Maybe your mom even
has a timer. Yikes. Here's the
best book for you:

This one. Right here!

This page is the

MOST IMPORTANT.

It is a list of rules.

Rule 1: Look at the book and move your eyes from side to side. Slowly. Eyes on book.

Rule 2: Stay in your seat. Butt on chair.

Rule 3: Repeat rules 1 and 2 over and over for 20 minutes or until a grown up says you're done. Eyes on book. Butt on chair.

Scene 3

Reading is not so bad when the words are easy. So this page is full of easy words.

To, I, and. To, I, and.
OK. OK. OK. OK. OK. OK.
No, no, no, no.

Oh yes, A.
A is an easy word, too.
It's the easiest of all. We can't forget A.

A, a, a, a, a, a, a, a.

Scene 4

Here are some really hard words. If you don't know what they say, just move your eyes from side to side. Side to side. Side to side. Butt on chair. Eyes on book.

Or, you can just skip it. Yeah, just skip it.

Archipelago.
Plateau.
Plutonium.
Photosynthesis.
Pathatookoo. (Tricked you, that's not a real word.)

Scene 5

Ah-ha! You turned the page!

OK. Here are some reading tips from **Henry**. Henry hates to read, so his tips will be good.

Tip 1. First, pretend you have to go to the bathroom. Bring the book with you into the bathroom. Tell your mom you were reading in there.

Tip 2. Pick a book that has big pictures and small sentences.

Tip 3. Humor. Funny books seem to go by fast.

Tip 4. Distract your parents. If they are really busy, they will not notice you are not reading.

Scene 6

You are still here? Wow, that is pretty good. Here are tips from **Arthur**:

Tip 1. When you are in the car, always read the signs you see. Read out loud. That way, your mom and dad will think you read all day long.

Note: If you are in a car, and your parents want you to read a book, do what I do and say you get car sick. Throwing up is a good way to stop reading.

P.S. Speaking of that, bloody noses work too. They are as good as throw-up.

Dedication

The dedication is usually at the beginning of a book. Or at the end. But we forgot and put it in the middle.

Dedicated to everyone who hates reading and the people who love them anyway.

Scene 8

The rest of **Arthur's** tips:

Tip 2. Stare. Stare at the page. If you stare long enough, you will seem to be reading.

Tip 3. Chores. Maybe your parents will let you do chores instead of reading. Washing the car is fun if it is not too cold outside.

Tip 4. Math. Do your math homework instead of reading. Hey, it's something.

2 + 2 = 4

Scene 9

"Confession from Henry"

Scene 10

Reminder:

👀 Eyes on book. Butt on chair.

👀 Eyes on book. Butt on chair.

👀 Eyes on book. Butt on chair.

Repeat for -20- minutes.

Scene 11

Try not to get caught **NOT** reading.

Here is Henry's story:

I got caught not reading once in first grade. I was just looking at the pictures in my book. Then the teacher, Miss Gonzalez, asked, "Henry, are you just looking at the pictures?" And I was. The pictures were real good.

I looked up at Miss Gonzalez, then I turned to a page with lots of words and I put my eyeballs back on the book.
She left me alone.

Scene 12

Didn't that feel good? You got to turn the page without having to read. I wish all books had blank pages like that here and there.

Scene 13

About the scenes in this book ...

What's the difference between a scene and a chapter? Scenes are in movies and chapters are in books.

We know. This is not a movie. But we like movies better. We bet you do, too.

That reminds us of another tip: Pretend your book is a movie.

Scene 14

Vacation Reading

If you are on vacation and your parents make you read, do what we do. After a long day of touring around, ask if you can lie down while you read. Ask your parents to lie down, too. You will probably all fall asleep.

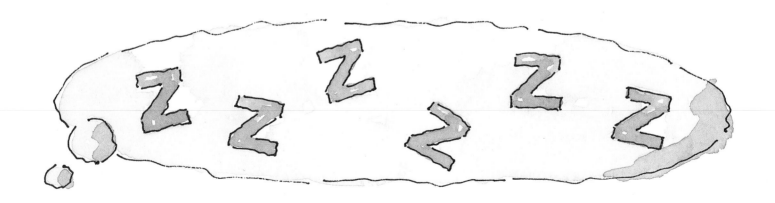

Scene 15

What to do about the kids at school who actually like to read.

Tip 1. Humor. Tell them a joke. Then tell them another and another. They will laugh and stop reading.

Tip 2. Shoes. Point out that their shoes are untied. This works for zippers too, even if their zippers are not down.

Tip 3. If your classroom has any man-eating animals, put the kids who like to read in the box with the man-eating animals. Without any books.

Scene 16

OK, we're done. Ah-ha! Tricked you! It's been -20- minutes. OK, maybe only 10. But you have been reading! You can't say you were just looking at the pictures because there aren't any.

The end.

Published by UpstartBooks
W5527 State Road 106
P.O. Box 800
Fort Atkinson, Wisconsin 53538-0800
1-800-448-4887

Text © 2008 by Arthur and Henry Bacon
Illustrations © 2008 by Johanna B. Hantel